Community Helpers at Work

A Day with a Librarian

By Katie Kawa

Cavendish Square
New York

Published in 2021 by Cavendish Square Publishing, LLC
243 5th Avenue, Suite 136, New York, NY 10016

Copyright © 2021 by Cavendish Square Publishing, LLC

First Edition

No part of this publication may be reproduced, stored in a retrieval system, or transmitted in any form or by any means—electronic, mechanical, photocopying, recording, or otherwise—without the prior permission of the copyright owner. Request for permission should be addressed to Permissions, Cavendish Square Publishing, 243 5th Avenue, Suite 136, New York, NY 10016. Tel (877) 980-4450; fax (877) 980-4454.

Website: cavendishsq.com

This publication represents the opinions and views of the author based on his or her personal experience, knowledge, and research. The information in this book serves as a general guide only. The author and publisher have used their best efforts in preparing this book and disclaim liability rising directly or indirectly from the use and application of this book.

Library of Congress Cataloging-in-Publication Data

Names: Kawa, Katie, author.
Title: A day with a librarian / Katie Kawa.
Description: New York : Cavendish Square Publishing, [2021] | Series: Community helpers at work | Includes index.
Identifiers: LCCN 2019045639 (print) | LCCN 2019045640 (ebook) | ISBN 9781502658180 (paperback) | ISBN 9781502658197 (set) | ISBN 9781502658203 (library binding) | ISBN 9781502658210 (ebook)
Subjects: LCSH: Librarians–Juvenile literature. | Libraries–Juvenile literature.
Classification: LCC Z682 .K27 2021 (print) | LCC Z682 (ebook) | DDC 020.92–dc23
LC record available at https://lccn.loc.gov/2019045639
LC ebook record available at https://lccn.loc.gov/2019045640

Editor: Katie Kawa
Copy Editor: Nathan Heidelberger
Designer: Andrea Davison-Bartolotta

The photographs in this book are used by permission and through the courtesy of: Cover Ekaphon maneechot/Shutterstock.com; p. 5 Bullstar/Shutterstock.com; p. 7 SW Productions/Stockbyte/Getty Images; pp. 9, 23 wavebreakmedia/Shutterstock.com; p. 11 David Brewster/Star Tribune via Getty Images; p. 13 ESB Professional/Shutterstock.com; pp. 15, 17, 21 Tyler Olson/Shutterstock.com; p. 19 SDI Productions/E+/Getty Images.

Some of the images in this book illustrate individuals who are models. The depictions do not imply actual situations or events.

CPSIA compliance information: Batch #CS20CSQ: For further information contact Cavendish Square Publishing LLC, New York, New York, at 1-877-980-4450.

Printed in the United States of America

CONTENTS

At the Library — 4

Using Computers — 14

Helping Everyone — 20

Words to Know — 24

Index — 24

At the Library

A library is a **special** place. It's full of books! A librarian is a person who works at a library. Librarians are very helpful. They help people find books to read. They help people in many other ways too.

People borrow books from the library. This means they take books home for a while. Then, they bring them back. A person needs a library card to borrow books. A librarian can help them get one.

Some libraries are very big! It can be hard to find the right book in a big library. Librarians know where to look. They answer questions about different kinds of books.

Libraries also have movies. People can borrow movies and watch them at home. A librarian helps people find the movies they want to watch. They help people find music too.

Librarians help kids learn and have fun. Libraries often have story time for kids. A librarian reads a story. Then, they help kids play a game or make a **craft**.

Using Computers

Librarians use computers to help them do their job. Computers help them keep track of books. They can use a computer to see if a book is at the library.

15

Libraries often have many computers. People visit the library to use the computers. Sometimes people need help using the computers.
They can ask a librarian. Librarians show people how computers work.

Some libraries have other fun things people can use. Many libraries now have 3-D printers. These are printers that make objects, such as boxes and toys. Librarians help people use 3-D printers.

Helping Everyone

Many schools have libraries. School librarians have an important job. They help **students** find books they need for their homework. They also help students find books to read for fun.

A librarian's day is often busy! They work hard to help people find what they need at the library. They also help people learn. Librarians help kids and adults. They make the library a fun place to visit!

23

WORDS TO KNOW

craft: An object made with a person's hands.

special: Different from others in a good way.

students: People who go to a school to learn.

INDEX

B
borrowing, 6, 10

C
computers, 14, 16
craft, 12

L
library card, 6

M
movies, 10
music, 10

S
schools, 20
story time, 12
students, 20